RURI'M Chicken

MARGERY CUYLER

PICTURES BY
PUY PINILLOS

ALBERT WHITMAN & COMPANY
CHICAGO, ILLINOIS

"Purim is coming," crowed Cock-a-Doodle-Doo.
"Time to rehearse our Purim songs," mooed Moo.
"And make groggers," bleated Bleat.
"And eat hamantaschen," baaed Baa.
"And wear costumes," neighed Neigh.
"For our Purim play," quacked Quack.

"May I have a crack at playing Queen Esther?" clucked Cluck.

Quack ruffled her feathers. She had always played the queen.
"I already know all the lines," she quacked.
The other animals nodded. "Maybe next year," they agreed.
"This just isn't my clucky day," Cluck clucked to herself.

That afternoon, the animals drew up the cast:

Quack: Queen Esther

Moo: Mordecai, Queen Esther's uncle

Neigh: Ahasuerus, the king of Persia

Baa: Vashti, the first wife of Ahasuerus and the Queen of Persia

Cock-a-Doodle-Doo: Haman, the evil prime minister

Honk, Hoot, Bleat, Cluck: the audience

"At least I have a part in the audience," clucked Cluck.
"That's better than nothing."

For several weeks, the animals rehearsed the story of Queen Esther and how she saved the Jews in Persia from the evil plans of Haman, the prime minister. The audience—Honk, Hoot, Bleat, and Cluck—honked, hooted, bleated, and clucked whenever Haman's name was mentioned.

But Cluck worried. What if her cluck wasn't loud enough to drown out Haman's name? She and the others had to create a lot of noise to remind everyone that he was wicked.

I'll just work on making my cluck louder, she decided. Cluck practiced every day.

And then practiced some more.

CLUCK!

Finally it was the day before Purim. Bleat made groggers by filling tin cans with pebbles. The animals made costumes out of the sheets on Farmer Ezra's clothesline. They borrowed a tray of hamantaschen from Farmer Ezra's kitchen.

But that afternoon, something terrible happened. Quack disappeared!

SPARKLY FEATHERS

"She has flown the coop!" crowed Cock-a-Doodle-Doo.

"How udderly terrible!" mooed Moo.

"This really gets my goat," bleated Bleat.

"What baaad luck!" baaed Baa.

"Hold your horses," neighed Neigh. "Let's send out a search party."

"I'll look down by the pond," clucked Cluck.

As Cluck scratched around in the mud, she saw some footprints. *The footprints of a fox!*

The other animals heard her loud clucks and came running. When they saw the footprints leading from the pond to the fence and from the fence to the woods, they began to crow, moo, bleat, baa, neigh, honk, and hoot.

"That wily fox has stolen our star!" crowed Cock-a-Doodle-Doo.

"Holy cow!" mooed Moo.

"I'll be brave like Queen Esther," clucked Cluck. "I'll find that fox and save our friend!" Off she flew, following the footprints across the field, through the woods...to Fox's den.

Cluck hid behind a rock. She saw Quack tied to a tree.
Fox was lighting a fire under a big pot nearby.

Oh no, thought Cluck. Fox plans to cook Quack for dinner!
I must try even harder to be brave like Queen Esther.

Cluck took a deep breath, pushed herself off the ground,
and flew like the wind toward Fox.

Duck à
L'Orange

1 Duck
2 Carrots
Celery
3 Leeks
2 oranges

CIVCK! CIVCK!

She squawked into his ear.

"Go away!" screeched Fox.

Cluck flew behind Fox. She pecked at his tail.

"Ouch!" howled Fox. "Ouch!"

"No more stealing from the barnyard," clucked Cluck.

"Or *you'll* be the one who's cooked for dinner!"

"I'm outta here!" cried Fox. He skedaddled toward the woods.

"You're a good egg," quacked Quack. "You saved me just in time. Otherwise I'd have been duck soup."

When they got back to the barnyard, Quack quack, quack, quacked out the story of Cluck's brave rescue.

"Hooray for Cluck!" crowed, mooed, bleated, baaed, neighed, honked, and hooted the animals.

"I have to duck out of the play tonight," quacked Quack. "I'm just too flustered to perform."

"What bad moos," mooed Moo. "Who can take your place?"

"How about Cluck?" quacked Quack.
"She would make a ducky queen!"

"A ducky queen and a *brave* queen," crowed, mooed,
bleated, baaed, neighed, honked, and hooted the animals.
"On with the show!"

So Cluck played Queen Esther after all! And the animals, especially Quack, agreed that she made an excellent Queen Esther indeed.

For Chris—MC
To Luis, the three musketeers, and little Samuel—PP

Library of Congress Cataloging-in-Publication data
is on file with the publisher.

Text copyright © 2017 by Margery Cuyler
Pictures copyright © 2017 by Puy Pinillos
Published in 2017 by Albert Whitman & Company
ISBN 978-0-8075-3381-9

Printed in the United States of America
10 9 8 7 6 5 4 3 2 1 LB 20 19 18 17 16

Design by Jordan Kost

For more information about Albert Whitman & Company,
visit our website at www.albertwhitman.com.